Spineless Wonders

PO Box 220

Strawberry Hills

New South Wales, Australia, 2012

https://shortaustralianstories.com.au

First published by Spineless Wonders 2021

Cover image copyright Bettina Kaiser

Editorial assistance by Jessica Duff, Melissa Woolley and Natalia Smith

Typeset in Adobe Garamond Pro

Printed and bound by Ingram Spark Australia
Slinkies 2021 An anthology of short stories
1st ed.

ISBN 978-1-925052-69-5 (pbk)

A catalogue record for this book is available from the National Library of Australia

Slinkies 2021

stories

Edited by

Emma Wortley, Elizabeth Mora & Deniz Agraz

spineless wonders

www.shortaustralianstories.com.au

Content

Introduction

Spineless Wonders Slinkies has been publishing new and emerging Australian writers under 30 since 2014, with short stories and novellas of all styles and genres. In 2021 there were over sixty entries from authors all across Australia and some Australian writers living overseas, and it was tough to choose just five pieces.

As in previous years, while some of the authors have a few publications or awards under their belt, others are being published and working with an editor for the first time ever.

So what will you find in this year's anthology? Three of the stories have a creeping sense of dread, in very different contexts. Two of the stories are preoccupied with the idea of making connections and how we can really know ourselves or others. While these themes always resonate, it particularly makes sense that these are the stories the editors were drawn to after the last tumultuous year.

We would like to thank Melissa Woolley and Jessica Duff for their assistance on this publication.

Happy reading!

Emma Wortley, Elizabeth Mora & Deniz Agraz

Dress Code

Amanda Jayne

Michael always chooses the same seat on his bus ride to work, the same mug from the kitchenette cupboard for his mid-morning tea and the same lunchtime salmon bagel from the deli across the road from his office. His polished Oxfords are his fourth pair from the same online wholesaler, and he has used the same brand of sandalwood shower gel for ten years. Tonight, he returns home to a foil-covered dinner plate, which he eats while his wife sips a peppermint tea and tells him she's booked tickets to visit her mother next month. It's a shame he can't join her, but it'll be better for her to go alone as he's a nervous flyer and isn't particularly fond of his mother-in-law.

After dinner, he takes his evening shower. He loosens his tie, undoes his belt and drapes his pants carefully over the towel rail. He tries to unbutton his shirt at the collar, but his fingers can't seem to find purchase. He pinches the fabric and presses so hard that the button leaves an angry imprint on his thumb. He turns on the vanity light above the sink, examines the rounded plastic surface and figures it must somehow be caught on a loose thread. He hunts through the bathroom cabinet for a pair of scissors, but all he can find are toenail clippers. He snips under the button for its attaching thread, but the clippers are uselessly curved. Frustrated, he drops them in the sink and his wife hears the clatter.

'Honey,' she calls from the bedroom, 'are you alright?'

'Fine.'

He searches the cabinet for a proper pair of scissors, peering behind his wife's perfume bottles and lipstick tubes.

'Do we have scissors somewhere?'

'What?'

'Scissors!'

He hears his wife get out of bed and pad across the floor. She knocks lightly.

'No, don't come in. Just tell me where they are, please?'

'Second draw from the bottom. On the left.'

'I can't find anything. You know I don't like it when you rearrange things without asking.' He kneels and reaches to the back of the drawer, shuffling his hand over spare packets of toothbrushes and bars of soap until he feels a cool hard edge. 'Found them!'

He straightens and watches closely in the mirror, guiding his hand in reverse as he positions the tip of the scissors around the button thread.

The scissors snip, but the thread remains intact. The button seems to gaze up at him innocuously.

'Alright, give me a hand, would you?' He unlocks the door. 'It's my top button. It won't come undone.'

'Come here,' his wife takes the scissors gently, and he tilts his head back for her to examine his collar. Frowning, she twists and presses at the button with her nails.

'It must be caught on something.' She tries snipping the thread, but when the scissors can't find their grip, she slips the blade into the gap between the buttons and cuts into the fabric of the shirt.

'Careful!'

'Trust me,' she says. 'You have others, and it's not coming off otherwise.' He feels the cool blade at his neck as she cuts through the collar.

'Ouch, Jesus! Be careful!'

She slices down and the shirt slithers from his shoulders, falling to the bathroom floor like a layer of shed skin.

His wife gasps and drops the scissors. He turns to the mirror and yells in fright at the sight of his upper body flushed bright red. A spot of blood blossoms at his neck, congealing in his chest hair.

'You cut me!'

'I didn't!'

'Well, how do you explain this?' Flustered, he bundles up his tattered shirt and stuffs it into the miniature bathroom bin. 'I must've had an allergic reaction to the shirt fabric. The button must've gotten stuck somehow. And you cut me with the scissors. Don't worry about that,' he snaps as she retrieves disinfectant and Band-Aids from the cabinet. His wife nods and returns to the bedroom, closing the door behind her.

Alone again, he examines his body more closely. He has never had an allergic reaction before. He wipes away the blood with a dampened square of toilet paper, brushes his teeth and swills a capful of mouthwash. He keeps his shower lukewarm so as not to aggravate the stinging rash and dries himself gingerly with a freshly laundered towel. His navy, silk pyjamas feel wonderfully cool against his skin.

By the time he emerges from the bathroom, his wife is already asleep with her hair spread across the pillow. He opens his closet and runs a hand along the shirts hanging in shades of white, beige and grey. He has worn the same cotton shirts to work every day, so he decides that some kind of pollen must have worked its way under his collar on his walk home from the bus stop. The pollen must have somehow caused his fingers to swell, hence his clumsiness with the buttons.

With the matter settled, he gets into bed beside his wife, turns off his bedside light, and waits for sleep.

***

The next morning, he shaves and dresses neatly in a grey suit and tie. His skin has returned to normal, aside from a scab of dried blood under his throat, and the buttons of his white cotton shirt slide into place without resistance.

He is in high spirits as he breakfasts with his wife in the kitchen, responding to emails while she serves soft scrambled eggs with warmed bread rolls and honey. He takes his usual seat on the bus and skims the documents that need to be reviewed ahead of his morning meeting. He reads emails on his phone as he walks through the lobby, rides the elevator typing one-handed replies, and hardly needs to look up from his screen to navigate to his desk. The day passes in an easy sequence of meetings and editing. The office empties and peak-hour traffic eases before he finishes and prints a thick sheaf of papers to mark up with his red editing pen. Back home, he hangs his jacket, unlaces his shoes and takes his work with him to the kitchen, where his dinner of lemon roasted chicken breast, potatoes and garlicy green beans awaits, wrapped in foil. He eats while crossing out sentences and writing neat corrections in the margins. His wife remains in the living room, reading a novel on the couch with a homemade gin fizz perspiring on the coffee table beside her.

His fingers aren't swollen and his skin feels normal under the shirt, but a deepening sense of dread keeps him at the kitchen counter with his red pen. Eventually, his wife clears away his plate and touches him softly on the shoulder.

'Coming to bed?' she asks.

'In a minute.' He draws a line through a paragraph.

'It's late,' she rests her head on his shoulder.

'Fine.' He leaves the papers scattered across the counter and follows his wife into the bedroom.

'I'll just take a shower,' he says, and his wife pretends not to notice the quiver in his voice.

He closes the bathroom door and turns the lock. He makes to loosen his tie, but his hands shake and he feels compelled to unbuckle his belt first. He undoes the clasp and removes his pants slowly, delaying as he folds and hangs them carefully over the towel rail.

His tie feels constricting around his neck as he hesitantly works a finger under the knot, before sharply pulling it loose and letting it slip to the floor in a coil.

He holds his breath and looks at the button, vibrating with his heartbeat. He knows, with sudden clarity, that he won't be able to take off his shirt. He tries the button half-heartedly, and when it won't slide through its hole he gives up and anxiously pulls his collar from side to side until his neck burns.

'Honey, are you alright?' His wife knocks and tries the handle.

'I'm fine,' he tries to keep his voice steady.

'Are you having trouble with your button again?' she asks.

He considers lying but instead unlocks the door.

'Let me—' she steps forward.

'No!'

'We'll have to get you some new shirts,' she says with resolve, and opens the drawer for the scissors.

'You'll cut me again.' He backs away towards the shower cubicle.

'How else are we going to get that shirt off you?' she implores, reaching for the hem of his shirt.

'No!' He darts past his wife and into the bedroom. She waits a moment for him to calm before she follows, finding him on the edge of the bed with his head in his hands.

'It won't come off,' he mumbles into his palms. 'I just know it.'

'Let me see.' His wife softens her voice and kneels in front of him. 'Trust me.'

He watches as she begins to lift the hem of his shirt.

'Ouch!' he yelps in pain and pushes her away.

'I barely touched you.'

'Just leave it.' He gets up from the bed and returns to the safety of the kitchen. He's not going to be able to fall asleep, so he might as well get some work done.

His wife curls up under the duvet and lies awake, waiting. When he returns to the bedroom and falls into bed, she kisses his cheek and tries to pretend that he isn't still wearing his work shirt.

***

As the weeks pass, he learns to wear his shirt like an outer layer of skin. At first, he worries that the shirt will become smelly with sweat, but he learns to use a gentle laundry wash in the shower and dries off with his wife's hairdryer. He trains himself to sleep with his back propped up against a pile of pillows, the fabric smoothed out beneath him so as not to wrinkle it.

Worried that any stains might become permanent scars, he is always careful to lean right over his plate and he avoids strongly pigmented foods. No more red wine with his steak, or coffee with his breakfast. He stops going to the gym but finds he doesn't miss the claustrophobic weights room, with its industrial fans and overhead television screens. On weekends, he pairs the shirt with dark wash jeans and enjoys the freedom from choice. Nobody, except his wife, notices that he hasn't changed in weeks. He donates a box of shirts and weekend polos to charity, and while the household washing pile has reduced by half, the permanent line between his wife's eyebrows only deepens.

***

The evening after his wife returns home from visiting her mother, she confronts him while he edits documents and snacks on handfuls of dried fruit in the kitchen.

'I've booked you in for tomorrow.'

She hands him an appointment card, with tomorrow's date and 10:30 a.m. handwritten beneath the embossed name and title of a clinical psychologist.

'I don't need this.' He flicks the card in the direction of the bin and returns to his work. His wife touches the back of his neck, right above his collar.

'Please,' she says. 'We both know this isn't normal.'

He gathers up his papers and makes for the front door. 'I can't get any work done here. I'm going to the office.'

'So late?'

'I need to have this finished by tomorrow morning.'

'You need to take off that shirt.'

'It's none of your business what I wear. I've never told you to get rid of those old college shirts of yours. Or those gaudy dresses you wear to the farmers' market.'

'Please, Michael, I just want to help you. You obviously have some kind of problem.'

'By whose definition? I'm getting up every day just fine, going to work, eating, sleeping—'

'But the shirt—'

'The shirt has nothing to do with it!' His cheeks flush with anger and shame.

'It's not hygienic,' she whispers, eyes downcast.

'Come here,' he says, and she shuffles towards him. He takes hold of her hand and guides it to his chest.

'See? It feels perfectly normal, and here,' he lifts an arm, but she wrinkles her nose and pulls away.

'I'm telling you: it doesn't smell.' Cautiously, she leans towards him and breathes in the lavender of their laundry detergent and the sandalwood of his shower gel.

'I'm fine,' he says firmly. 'In fact, I'm glad. Think how much time I'm saving in the morning. Sure, I've had to make a few minor lifestyle adjustments, but my days are so much easier. In fact, it's really helping me to stay in the right mindset for my work. Do you know what my manager told me today?'

She shakes her head.

'He's considering putting me up for Allen's job when he retires next year. Says I'm a shoo-in if I keep going as I am.'

His wife looks up at him and he smiles at her.

'Trust me, sweetheart, it's going to be fine. Better than fine.'

'I guess,' she says, 'as long as you're happy.'

'It's not a question of happiness,' he says. 'It's just who I am.'

The Last Fence

Vasco Pimentel

She sat on her front porch as her nephew played with the dogs, fighting over a jarrah stick. A cup of instant coffee warmed her palms in a winter morning like many others. She admired the horizon from the porch, a framed picture of dry plains contrasted by a blue and grey sky carrying promises of welcome rain. The kelpies ran around, full of purpose, trying to find the stick amid the knee-high vegetation. A chicken coop watched the dogs' every move with minute attention and would startle if the stick was thrown in their direction. Myrtle thought these chickens must have experienced this same dance of danger every day of their existence, but still jumped around frenetically every time one of the kelpies came close. Whenever let loose they seemed more confident in their movements, but when put back behind that same wire fence their tiny little hearts would beat a tad faster.

The dogs came to a halt. The hair on their backs grew thicker and their tails rose sharply as their radar detected something unusual. Her nephew's reaction to the dogs told her something was off.

'Get over here,' she said. 'Lock the barn and bring your father's Winchester.'

The nephew put his head down and ran to the barn, followed closely by both dogs, who also awaited instructions. She took a pensive sip from her cup as the noise of an engine echoed in the distance. A long cloud of smoke rose as a white vehicle ploughed through the dryness of what was left of the road leading to the farm. She thought about covering the embers used to cook breakfast, but it was too late now. The smoke left the chimney in an upward dance of freedom. Jack came back gasping for air and handed the rifle to his auntie.

'Keep on playing with the dogs,' she told him. 'It's a normal day and we don't want them too startled.'

The nephew jumped down from the porch, his head down as he tried to find the jarrah stick.

'Coppers,' he said, looking ahead, holding the stick as he tried to keep the dogs busy.

The chequered vehicle slowed down before the fence around the farmhouse. It seemed to hesitate for a second as its wheels stopped outside the gate. Her stomach rumbled as she concentrated on not spilling what was left of her coffee. She finally stood up, finished her cup, picked up the rifle and made her way to the gate with a slow but confident pace.

Both men in the vehicle watched in silence as Myrtle made her way to the fence and leaned her foot on the wire, rifle over her shoulder. She tucked her silvering hair behind her ears and put her brother's old hat on. The men turned the engine off and rolled down the window on the driver's side.

'How do you do, ma'am?' the driver asked. Myrtle let the question linger like the dust that hung behind the truck. 'Is this your property?' She merely squinted her eyes, trying to see through the dark masks and helmets the officers wore. 'We've been asked to come and see you to collect your ration tax.'

Myrtle whistled and signalled her nephew to let the dogs come closer. Both the kelpies ran towards the fence and sat next to the farmer. She looked up and said, 'Only thing you'll be collecting around here is bullet holes if you don't turn back now and get off my property.'

The men exchanged a brief look, and the second officer opened his door. He moved with assurance, as if taking pride in the huge footprint left by his right military boot when stepping out of the truck. Myrtle swallowed deep and felt her hand tighten around the rifle's wooden grip. The dogs also swallowed in anticipation but held their ground. The officer closed the door, contemplated the horizon, and made his way to the fence. As he edged closer, Myrtle noticed he had no name tag on. *A bully in a mask,* she thought.

'Miss, when was the last time you paid your tax? We're in a state of emergency.'

'From ma'am to miss. That didn't take long. May I see your badge?'

'Ma'am,' the man looked back at his colleague in the car and kept on going, 'all farmers are being asked to contribute to society in this state of emergency, and that includes you. What exactly do you produce on this farm?'

'Society?' she looked back and gave Jack a smile, who stood by the porch. 'When all this madness started, society left us here for dead.

And now that we have fended for ourselves, you come to my property asking for help? Don't think so, mate.'

'We aren't asking. Martial law is in place, ma'am.' He undid the holster on his handgun. 'Is the man of the house home?'

Myrtle cocked the lever on her Winchester and looked him in the eye.

'Right in front of you.' A crow landed on the fence next to them. The policeman looked around the green house behind Myrtle, and she could see a smile in his blue, needle-sharp eyes. 'Show me your badge so I can send you on your way, officer.'

He snapped. 'Listen here, you fuckin' bitch, you are going to open that fuckin' gate for us, and if you're lucky, we'll let you and farmer boy there live. Do you get me? Open that fucking gate right now.'

The crow cawed, as if entertained. The kelpies started growling, running up and down the fence. Myrtle took a long look at the driver who pulled his mask down to light a cigarette, revealing a tattoo of a tear drop under his right eye.

'Right fuckin' now, missy.' Myrtle took a deep breath and gazed back at the porch as if weighing her options. Jack was gone. The masked man seemed fuelled by this and reached for his gun. 'Why do you make me repeat myself?'

The dogs ran up and down the fence. She took a last look at the driver who smiled with a cigarette between his teeth. His partner was pulling the gun out, still smiling, as he said:

'Every. Fuckin'…'

A loud bang broke the silent morning and the crow flew away. The chickens fluttered around in their coop. Myrtle lunged into the dry vegetation as the masked officer collapsed across the fence, the dogs barking frantically as if celebrating a victory. The driver turned on the engine as fast as he could, smile and cigarette both gone from his mouth. He sped away, leaving a cloud of dust behind.

'Jack!' she yelled, looking around for her nephew, who came running with a rifle in tow. 'Are you alright?' she asked him, grabbing him by the shoulders. His eyes were focused across the fence, his pupils in a frenetic dance.

'I got him,' he said. 'I got him.'

A mix of adrenaline and terror ran through Myrtle as she lunged across the fence. The kelpies stuck their noses between the wire, their tails wagging with excitement. Jack stood his ground, holding the rifle in awe as if still grasping its full power.

She leaned over the masked officer, whose blue eyes were now almost completely dark. Blood gushed from the side of his throat as the mask covered the surprise on his face. Myrtle looked around. 'Jack! Bring him to the barn,' she said. 'They might come back for him.'

***

Jack dragged the masked man with the help of his auntie as the dogs sniffed the stranger with fascination. Myrtle saw the marks left behind in the dirt by the man's boots and remembered the hot summer night when her brother had collapsed by the chicken coop. She had had to drag him to the barn for both their sakes, and the vividness and resemblance of the situation brought her some less than fond memories of that late summer. The consequences of the virus were still unknown back then, and Myrtle reflected on the true function of wearing a mask as they dragged the stranger to the old barn.

'Is he gonna be alright?' Jack asked as he opened the barn door. The sweat running down his forehead enhanced the bright light brown in his eyes, along with his jovial scruffy curls which stuck to his tanned brow.

'It's hard to tell. The bullet seems to have gone straight through, but the last thing we need around here is another mouth to feed.'

They tied the man to one of the barn's central beams, the chain engulfing his torso like an anaconda's embrace. Myrtle lit up a blowtorch against her dad's old scythe. The incandescent metal breathed a warm smell as she saw Jack kneeling in front of the stranger to get a sense of his identity. He motioned to unmask the man but was stopped by his auntie:

'Step back. This man is not your friend. I don't want you anywhere near him unless I say so.'

Jack stood back and petted the dogs, his fascinated eyes glowing with acknowledgment as his auntie turned off the blowtorch and approached the man with the incandescent scythe.

'Do you understand me, Jack?'

She looked him in the eyes before holding the searing metal to the man's wound. A comforting smell filled the barn with a sizzling sound, contrasted by the man's loud yelling. He opened his eyes in a mixture of panic and surprise to see the woman holding a blazing blade to his throat. Both the shock and pain sent him back to sleep as Myrtle removed the blade and analysed the bullet wound.

'That will have to do for now,' she said, as she threw the scythe back into one of the metal crates. Her nephew watched the scene in fascination along with the dogs who sniffed the man's boots with precaution.

'Come on Jack, we have work to do.'

He looked up the same way a child does when told dinner time has interrupted playtime with a new toy. Myrtle put her arm around her nephew as they walked away from the man.

'Here's what I need from you: double check the rifles in case someone comes back for him.

Double-check the gate, I don't want anyone in or out. Keep an eye out; and if you see something, come straight for me. Got it?'

'What about him?' he asked, observing the man over his auntie's shoulder.

'Don't worry about him. He's not going anywhere. Now go.'

Both Jack and the dogs left in an excited hurry. Myrtle found herself alone with the man in the peacefulness of the barn. She made sure the chain was tight enough and allowed herself to breathe. *It's just another day*, she thought. Better get to work.

She locked the barn's great wooden doors and was once again brought back to that same summer night that had changed the farm's balance forever. The barn had seen its share of unwelcome guests. But this was no time for reminiscing. Myrtle shook the thought off and made her way to the farmhouse.

The rest of the day went on like any other. They worked the fields, cleaned the coop and fed the pigs; only difference being the presence of the rifles as a reminder of the danger outside those fences.

Myrtle pondered whether she should light a fire to warm the farmhouse. She thought about the unexpected visit that morning and decided it would not make a difference. Better dying warm than living a life of fear. She sent Jack and the dogs out to gather some firewood and started preparing dinner.

The stillness in the farmhouse was filled by the cracking sound of the firewood, which helped her think. Who were these people? What if they really were police officers? Was martial law really in place? What went on outside those fences? Myrtle struggled to decide whether she would like to find out and kept chopping the chicken away, the bang of the knife against the wooden board slowing the pace of her frantic thoughts. Jack came running and panting and her grip on the knife stiffened instantly.

'He's awake! He's awake!' he yelled through the flyscreen.

Myrtle dropped the knife and rushed towards the barn.

'What were you doing in there?' she asked him, while the dogs followed her chicken-drenched fingers with amused curiosity.

'The axe was in there, auntie, I swear. He was asleep when I came in, but I think one of the dogs woke him up.'

They stopped before entering the barn. She put both her hands on his shoulders and said:

'You did well.' She took a deep breath. 'You're a good kid, Jack. Remember that. Now tend to that fire and make sure you don't burn the house down.'

He hesitated for a second but made his way back towards the farmhouse with the axe in tow. Myrtle watched him and took another deep breath before the great wooden doors. She entered. The man was in a trance-like state but looked awake. He startled as she came in and tried to free himself, to no avail.

'You crazy bitch! Where am I?'

'I should ask you the same question. Do you know where you are? Why did you come here?'

He tried to focus his gaze on Myrtle, as if to decipher the farmer's intentions. Myrtle also took a good first look at the unwonted visitor and tried to paint his picture. She deduced him to be in his mid-twenties, eager and young, and his shaved crew-cut head reminded her of her late brother's military days. She saw in him the same look you get when enclosing a wild animal for the first time.

'You've lost a lot of blood. But the wound seems to be healing alright. You're a lucky man. A couple of centimetres to the right and you would've been dead. But you're not in the clear just yet. I'll urge you to choose your answers very carefully if you want to part with that beam.'

She dragged her feet through the hay as he observed her every move. She picked up the scythe from the metal box and walked towards him. His breathing started speeding out of his lungs as the fear constricted the chain around his chest. She edged closer.

'What is your name, stranger, and why have you come to my farm?'

His eyes took on an agitated dance between the scythe and Myrtle's dark, steely gaze, as if both were asking the question.

'I'm Mac. You don't know what it's like out there.'

'Well Mac, I'm hoping you can tell me all about it, otherwise I don't have much use for you now, do I?'

'Yes ma'am.' He swallowed deep. Sweat poured from his brow, leaving tracks of washed blood down his face. 'Give me some water and I'll tell you all I know.'

'Tell me now and I'll get you some. Why are you wearing a mask? How dangerous is this thing?'

'It's supposed to help stop the disease, but no one knows anymore. If there's no one around to spread it to, what's the point?'

Myrtle almost took a step back upon hearing the word *spread*, but held her ground as she felt no outsider information could corrupt their pristine fences.

'Why did you come here?'

'We saw the smoke.'

'Who is we? How many more of you?'

The man started dozing off. Myrtle stuck the scythe into the beam above the man's head.

'I dunno, a few…'

His face started losing colour as he struggled to stay awake. Myrtle observed the scene and pondered whether she was buying the act. She filled a bowl and drowned the thirsty man in water. His blue eyes dwelled on hers, now she was close. Her sun-kissed wrinkles gave her a sense of rough yet ruthless wisdom. He coughed the water towards her and observed her reaction.

'This thing is gonna get you if you keep on getting close. You're better off releasing me now.'

'You're not going anywhere until you answer my questions.'

She stood up and made her way towards the door. Mac's energy seemed to come back as he lost his cool and yelled in desperation:

'Don't leave me here, you fuckin' bitch! They're gonna get you! You won't make it to sunset tomorrow!'

You dumb motherfucker, Myrtle thought as she observed the man on her way out the door.

'I got a dinner to cook, *Mac*.' She smiled, giving him a final look before locking the great wooden doors behind her.

She came back to the house where her nephew was tending to the fire. She watched him from outside the flyscreen for a moment. What a long year it had been for both of them. Jack seemed to be healing day by day. The youngster, almost a man now, had grown a lot since his father's absence. The lack of constant judgement helped him thrive, even if at his own pace. She saw a lot of her brother in him and truly believed that one day he would be able to man the farm on his own. One day.

She tried to shake the image of her brother during that still summer night but to no avail. The image was perpetuated in her memory like a bad tattoo. How he had collapsed after dinner, the dinner she had cooked especially for him. How he used to yell at his son and call him *slow*. How the end of a bottle was never enough to dull the painstaking pace of life around the farm. And how he had never quite been the same since the war. She thought about Jack and how one should strive to be slow around here. Why speed up the inevitable?

Myrtle opened the flyscreen and took a last look at the wooden barn, a shiver running through her body as she thought to herself: *summer is over now*.

***

A metallic clutter in the kitchen stirred Myrtle from her sleep. As her feet touched the cold floorboards, she experienced an eerie yet reassuring lack of agency over her own movements. She watched herself walk through the corridor to the kitchen threshold to find Michael, her brother, opening cupboards and flipping plates and pots. The urgency in his manic gaze showed a need to find the solution to his every problem hiding behind the right door.

'Michael?' she heard herself ask. 'What are you up to? You're gonna wake Jack up.'

Michael's eyes quickly locked onto his sister's, before glancing towards an empty whisky bottle on the table as if to answer her question.

'Where is it?' he asked as his delirious pillaging resumed.

'I don't know what you're talking about,' Myrtle said.

The dreamy pace at which everything unfolded was quickly distorted as Michael lunged himself towards his sister and grabbed her by the neck.

'Where … is it?'

His cold grasp on her neck managed to squeeze out a single defeated word.

'Barn…'

The cold wooden floors embraced her once more as Michael released his grip and kicked the flyscreen on his way out. Myrtle recovered her breath and looked up along the corridor. She saw Jack peering out of his bedroom door with a scared yet puzzled look in his eyes.

'Go to bed, sweetheart… Everything is fine.'

Jack's door let out a comforting creak as he closed it. Myrtle allowed herself a deep breath and closed her eyes. As she did, she was brought back to the comfort of her warm bed. She sat up and grabbed her neck as if to make sure she really was awake. Myrtle knew her subconscious was playing tricks on her, but as with almost everything else in life, she knew nothing happened for no reason. That had been the night she'd decided on her unwonted course of action; a cold summer night which would come to change their lives forever. She'd learnt to trust her instincts, and had immediately grasped what her brain was trying to tell her: to reinstate the farm's balance.

***

Mac opened his eyes and saw Myrtle kneeling before him, her sombre gaze contoured by two wide, dark circles.

'You must be hungry,' she said.

'Fuckin' oath! And I need a piss too.'

'There is a big difference between what you want, and what you need. Between those two stands my goodwill. Now, I will ask you a series of questions, and whether you starve sitting on your own shit and piss is up to you. Do you get me, Mac?' Myrtle smiled at the end of the sentence, reluctant to accept Mac as his real name, but nevertheless entertained by the choice.

'Yes ma'am. Whaddya wanna know?'

'First of all, who was that other guy with you, and how did you get your hands on a police truck?'

'That fuckhead is my older brother, who left me here for dead. And no, there aren't any others, it's just me and my brother, like it's always been.'

'Are you sure, *Macca*?' Her inquisitive gaze saw right through him. He looked over her shoulder to see Jack peering by the door, the morning light bringing a welcome breath of life into the barn.

'Yes, I'm fuckin' sure. We found the truck in one of the little towns on the way here, the one with all the fuckin' fake plastic cows. Keys in the ignition and all. A whole town left for dead, a fuckin' police station left behind, only the fuckin' cows to keep watch. Some surreal shit, I'll tell you that. But I need a fuckin' piss ma'am, please! I beg you.'

'I'll get you a bottle, but we're only getting started here, Mac.'

'Sure, just get me fuckin' something, please!'

She passed the man a bottle and made sure he had enough leverage to use his weak hand.

'Now, I'm gonna cook some breakfast, and I don't want you to get any ideas now that you can move around a bit. The wound seems to be healing alright, but both those kelpies will tear your ankles to pieces if you decide to run. And besides, there is nothing around in the radius of at least ten Ks.'

She left the barn and posted Jack and the dogs to keep an eye on Mac. When she came back with the scrambled eggs, both her nephew and the dogs were in the exact same position. She set a plate just out of Mac's reach and sat on an old milking stool, her breakfast in hand, ready to get chatting. He broke the silence.

'What's with the kid? Does he think he's one of the dogs or something?'

She looked over to see Jack mowing through the breakfast he shared with the kelpies. That never failed to warm her heart.

'Something like that. Now, I might just set you free after brekkie if you tell me everything you know. What's with this ration tax?'

'Me and my brother came up with that to try and get some food off some farmers. First thing to happen out there were the shortages. People were almost killing each other over a piece of meat. Everyone got told to stay home until this thing was over. But no one will stay home if they're hungry, so people started jumping each other for food. It became eat or be eaten. That's what happened to me and my brother, we got fuckin' robbed overnight and barely got away.'

'It's not a good feeling, is it?' she asked him as she pushed the plate of eggs towards his left hand.

'We're just trying to survive out here, mate.' He started mowing through his breakfast, bits of yellow falling out of his mouth as he kept on going. 'Not everyone is set like you guys here, and I'll be fucked if they give you anything for free.'

'We've had our share to get where we are Mac, but we never had to steal from anyone.'

'It's the end of the fuckin' world as we know it, ma'am. A total mindfuck. Prices skyrocketed and jobs vanished. A group of madmen saw the opportunity and took it. First, they got to the news corps, then the internet and not long afterwards all phone lines were gone. Before you knew it, that group had become an organisation. They urged people to come back to reality, to stop behaving like fuckin' cows on the way to a slaughterhouse and start living their lives for themselves, or something along those lines. I wasn't one of them so I can only tell you what I heard. All I know is it's fuckin' mayhem out there.'

'Every man for himself. Sounds like pure order to me,' she said.

'Maybe I should learn something from you. But I will promise you this, ma'am,' he set his fork down and locked his blue gaze on hers, 'if you let me go, you'll never see me again.'

She looked back over her shoulder to see if her nephew was still about. His focus was still set on finishing the plate with the kelpies. She took her hat off and brushed her short hair behind her ears.

'We're at a crossroads here, Mac.' She paused, looking at her boots as the hay crumbled beneath them. 'I never planned on releasing you. But you seem like an honest young man, trying to get by. The illusion of a rug you sat comfortably on, all your life, has been swept right from under you. And this is where I urge you to make an important choice, the same way I have to make one.'

He swallowed deep as if this were his last meal.

'Now, if I let you go, you'll have a tough time out there making it back to wherever you crawled from. You'll struggle, but it will be *your* struggle, and no one can take that away from you.' Myrtle let that sentence linger in the stillness of the barn and took another mouthful of eggs. She wiped the edge of her mouth with her sleeve and kept going. 'If I don't let you go, you'll be confined to this barn for the rest of your frail existence. You'll work hard and be fed, but this is where you'll sleep every night, locked in a barn where I am the only one holding the key.'

She finished her eggs and let the young man think. Mac mulled over his options, his left hand brushing his eyebrow as if to help him think.

'What would you choose?' she asked, putting her empty plate down next to her.

'I mean, the eggs are pretty good…'

Jack ran outside with the dogs, bored by the long conversation. Mac gazed over Myrtle's shoulder, the morning horizon spreading as far as his mind could perceive. The endless blue ahead brought him a sense of peace.

'I guess I could stay, if you'd have me, ma'am,' he said, at last.

She picked up the plates and got up to leave. Mac was caught off guard by this and said:

'So? Where are you going? Will you let me stay? Please don't leave me in here!'

'It looks like you are eager to get onto the same sort of rug that swept you off your feet. I'm releasing you tonight. You'll have a long journey ahead of you. Get some rest.'

***

She prepared dinner by the fire and was once again brought back to that same nostalgic sense of peace with oneself she had adopted during that late summer night. The quietness of the farm at dusk helped her think, and the echoes of the past still hung around these walls. *They always will*, she thought. It had been under similar circumstances she had cooked her brother his last meal, and she was now doing the same for the stranger tied in the barn. *Like cows to a slaughterhouse*, Mac had said. And yet, when offered an opportunity to live again, a chance at the purest of freedoms, he had resigned to a life of subservience yet again. *Maybe we really are animals*, she thought, *and deserve to be treated as such*.

Myrtle reached over the cupboard where the final ingredient to Mac's meal had laid hidden since summer. She looked across the room to see Jack sleeping by the fire. Her rugged hands moved precisely as she spread the white powder through her final display of hospitality, a chicken sandwich. She wrapped it up in a piece of cloth. The small recipient where the powder laid hidden was put back in its place. Deep breath.

She opened the door to see a sunset of warring brushstrokes of red and grey. *He will still be able to walk for a few hours tonight*, she thought. A murder of crows cawed as it flew overhead. One of the kelpies followed her to the barn as she opened the wooden door. Mac had a confused look in his eyes when she came in.

'Hold this,' Myrtle said as she put the wrapped meal in his left hand.

She picked up the scythe and undid the chain. Mac struggled to get up at first, but when he did, he made sure he did not make any sudden movements. He looked back.

'Thank you for this. You'll never see me again, I promise.'

'Don't worry, I believe you. Now go, before I change my mind.'

She followed him with the scythe in hand, dog by her side. The man moved clumsily, as if he had never expected to walk again. A crow dangled in the wire-fence as Mac leaped over it. He looked back to see the woman standing by the fence, dog beside her. He raised his mask and stowed the sandwich in his jacket, ready to start the long journey ahead. He never looked back.

Myrtle walked back towards the house and sat on the porch, petting the dog. The sunset had now disappeared into the horizon. She watched as the stars lit up amid the clouds. A lonely spectator with her favourite seat in the house. *Just another day*, she thought, as she went inside to finish preparing dinner.

The Neighbours Are Curious

Morgan Riley

I

The kitten on the fence is pure energy. For the cockroach, timing is everything: the avoidance of death. The chase has enticed the kitten six or seven hundred meters away from its home, across Macquarie Fields to an unfamiliar backyard much bigger than its own—an enormous distance for a four-week-old kitten who has rarely ventured beyond its fibro house. It didn't mean to travel so far. The cockroach just wouldn't relent.

On this side of Macquarie Fields, the houses are invariably newer, sturdier brick structures surrounded by neatly trimmed Sir Walter Buffalo or Eureka grass. Rose gardens or supplanted native shrubs line the fences. Sometimes, in other backyards the kitten will explore later, a blue pool edged in pale limestone invites neighbourhood cats down from the fence for a drink.

The kitten, distracted by the chase, hasn't noticed the changing houses nor the unfamiliar people living inside them. People like the husband and wife in the living room, talking excitedly over one another, planning renovations for their new home as the kitten wobbles along the fence. They're still animated when they slide open the glass door at the back of the house.

Alerted by the sound, the kitten freezes in mid-stride, eyes already a little too large for its head and growing larger. The cockroach makes a final desperate surge. It scrabbles down the fence, sprints on tiny needling legs across the dirt and is safe in its home among the disappearing rockery. The husband and wife haven't seen the cat yet. They're focused on a spot of wood rot in the old decking, the next project after removing the rockery.

The kitten was born under a fibro house propped up on one side by clefted bricks that need replacing. From birth, it already knew the sound of doors, voices, footsteps. Sometimes doors lead to food; that was how the man who lives alone in the fibro house coaxed the kitten out from under the house after its mother disappeared. So when the cat hears the verandah door open and a man's familiar tenor talking excitedly, it waits, forepaw dangling, a tableau of a sneaking thief caught in floodlights.

But it's the woman who sees the kitten first. She crosses the verandah and descends the steps to the grass then comes forward towards the kitten slowly, one beckoning hand outstretched, making *ps-ps-ps* noises which the kitten obstinately ignores. It replaces its paw on the fence and braces. She stops, thinking she is scaring the animal, but it's the high-pitched wailing swelling from somewhere behind the couple that raises the kitten's hackles.

The kitten looks down at the man, who disappeared briefly but has come back outside with the shrieking thing bundled in his arms. High on the fence, the kitten is alert and confident, like a tapestry stitched with threads of soft fire. It watches for a while, trying to make sense of the rising wail that is so at odds with the things it knows, forgetting the cockroach, remembering the fibro house.

Then it turns and walks away

II

The kitten sniffs the air, trying to understand why this fence, this backyard, might be familiar. It's been a busy month: learning to pounce, practising on anything that moves, landing the target without being detected. There were uncountable new sensations and longer adventures beyond its own weedy lot on the western edge of Macquarie Fields. The cat is constantly rewriting the map in its head, adjusting to every tiny change.

The man's hearty laugh breaks through its reverie. The kitten shakes out first one leg then the other, and sits confidently on the fence, but the afternoon sun silhouettes its skinny frame in a shock of orange fur, betraying its big secret. It hardly strikes as a fearsome vermin hunter, more an oversized Myrtaceae, and the man can't hold back a chuckle.

"Hi there, little ginger," he calls across the backyard. "I thought we'd scared you off for good last month. You hungry? You look hungry. You wait a sec, little ginger, I'll be back."

A glass bottle clangs discordantly on a glass table when the man stands to go inside. He disappears through the open door, and the cat decides not to wait for the shrieking creature to come out again. Besides, something small and brown—a cockroach or a beetle, things the cat has become more adept at pouncing on—is scurrying across the grass in the next backyard. The kitten only has a momentary advantage. It coils, focuses, and scrabbles down the fence. Moments later, the man emerges through the door into an empty backyard.

III

From the other side of the double-glazed verandah door, the little ginger cat—no longer a kitten, not an adolescent yet—can only hear muffled voices. It lays in a rough semicircle of compressed earth where the rockery used to be, eyes closed, head resting on outstretched paws. The sliding door opens and two voices swell above several others. The cat's ears swivel towards the sound like tiny triangular satellite dishes aflame in the afternoon sun.

"I just don't see why you have to send them away," says the woman. Her voice doesn't bother the cat anymore, but it's not comforting like the man's gentle tenor.

"I'm not sending them away," says the man. "They're ready to go."

"Bullshit! We were having fun. Then you had to go and ruin it like you always do. You're such a killjoy when you're not the centre of attention."

"What? Look, you've been drinking since the morning. We'll let them leave and take it easy for the rest of the afternoon. Ok?"

The woman turns on her heel, going inside and sliding the door closed hard behind her. Startled, the cat springs up to a safer vantage point on the fence.

The man doesn't say anything right away. He just stands on the decking looking up into the afternoon sun, at the cat or somewhere past it. He takes a few deep breaths.

"Hey, little ginger," he calls, sweeping leaves off the new decking with his feet. He looks at the cat, puzzling something out. "You're not so little anymore," he says. The cat cocks its head and remains still.

Suddenly, a Willie Wagtail makes a daring pass a little too close and the cat's head whips around, but the bird gets away before the cat can move. It lands on the other side of the fence, in a particularly wormy patch of unkempt lawn. The voices swell again. When the cat looks back, the man is gone.

IV

The cat will sometimes visit the backyard when its adventures around Macquarie Fields lead that way, and if the afternoon sun provides a warm patch to rest, it might drop down for a while. Sometimes the family is home, and sometimes not. It doesn't matter much to the cat.

Half-asleep under a spring sun, the cat turns over and stretches, feeling freshly cut blades tickling its belly. It nearly falls asleep several times. But each time, the woman or man calling out, or the young boy's giggling, buoys it back to awareness. Enough time has passed that the cat doesn't recognise the wailing creature from its first visit when it was just a bottlebrush with bones. The boy, too, is bigger, but still unsteady on his feet.

The cat opens one eye when it senses someone—two people, one bigger than the other—approaching. "You have to be gentle, ok? Our little ginger friend might run away otherwise," says the man. The boy, barely heavy enough to make an indent in the springy Buffalo grass, approaches silently with wide-eyed awe. There's a moment suspended inside a swirling breeze; the cat, wary but not tensed, looks up at the boy who sways unsteadily on bare feet.

"Remember, be gentle," says the man, laying his hand on the boy's shoulder. The boy squats down and reaches out. The cat sniffs at the air and tenses. It doesn't recoil, so the boy touches the base of its neck, light enough that he only feels fine hair and not the muscle underneath. "That's the way, mate," says the man. "Good job. Nice and gentle." The man's voice reassures the cat. Three, four, five more strokes, and the boy is quivering with nervous energy, rocking a little, so when he looks up at his father, he overbalances, leaning awkwardly on the cat to stop from toppling over. There is no malice in the cat's departure, but maybe a little indignation. It stands, walks a few steps, shakes grass and the boy's handprint from its fur and trots to the fence. It leaps up and over and is gone.

The boy often watches the fence, waiting for the cat to come back. The cat has an entire sprawling suburb of backyards to discover, each one a shifting constellation of sensations contained within a galaxy of incomprehensible scale. On the other hand, the boy is just beginning to explore his expanding world. Mostly he ventures out with his parents, but the backyard is his own microcosm to conquer. So he watches the fence.

Sometimes the boy's parents watch the fence too, albeit with less wonder about where the cat goes, and more concern for all the other things coming and going in their lives. Mostly they're too busy to think about the infrequent visitor at all.

V

In the languid serenity of a late summer evening, the air in Macquarie Fields seems heavy with static electricity. A teasing Willie Wagtail and a daring chase traversing fences, roads and rooftops draw the cat back to a backyard it recognises; neat grass and a sandpit on one side, unkempt lawn and weeds on the other. A burr lodged in the cat's paw lets the bird escape unharmed, but the cat is nonplussed; it knows by the fading light that it will soon be dinner time at the blue fibro house.

So it nibbles the burr from its forepaw and watches the backyard below, where the little boy is playing alone, leaping up and down the decking stairs and cackling in the unrestrained alto kids learn in their first years of school. He happens to look up into the veil of oncoming dusk and see the cat watching him from the fence.

"Hey, little ginger!" he calls, breaking into a grin and walking fast towards the fence. The cat waits for a beat of contemplative stillness, then turns and strides away.

VI

The cat coils, ready to make a leap it has made dozens of times. Nobody is watching the fence; the boy outgrew that habit months earlier. Nearly a year has passed since the cat found its way to visiting the family, and the days are shorter and cooler, but even on a damp autumn afternoon the cat doesn't need to think too hard to stick the landing. Right before it springs up, a sliding door slams closed with enough force to send a ripple through the cat's stomach. The cat flattens its ears and crouches low. Copper fur bristles.

"I don't care. He's old enough to understand what's happening," says a woman's voice. "He's not a baby anymore. He sees it and hears it."

"Only because you're practically screaming," says a man's voice.

"Me? Screaming? How f— dare you. How. Dare. You. *You're* the one yelling and throwing things for no reason. *You're* the one who broke the phone last week, or have you already forgotten that?"

"Jesus, I'm surprised you remember that, you were so f— drunk."

"Oh, sure, *I* have a drinking problem, but *you* don't have an anger problem."

"Would you keep your voice down? We have neighbours, you know."

"Like I give a s—. They hear it all anyway. Hey, neighbours, did you hear him punch a hole in the door? Did you hear the remote shatter into a thousand tiny pieces because he couldn't get off his fat arse to change the volume?"

"Nice. Real nice."

The cat uncoils and abandons the fence. It turns towards the fibro house instead and is followed by the voices over two more fences. As it crosses a street to check on a bird nest it spied earlier, a door thuds closed somewhere behind.

VII

Unusually muggy winter weather drapes a thin fog over Macquarie Fields. The cat has been hunting through different backyards all morning, chasing all the things that come out on humid mornings. Now it sits on the fence, watching the woman and boy move around in the backyard, picking things up and taking them away. They sit together on the step or go in and out of the house. If either of them sees the cat, they don't greet it, and at some point they don't come back out from the house. Doors open and close. A car rumbles to life.

Weeds are beginning to claim some patches in the backyard, not to the point of making the house look derelict just yet. The cat watches a monstrous cockroach moving slowly through the long grass. It bounds silently off the fence and walks awkwardly through the backyard, lifting its paws to shake off moisture with each step until the cockroach wizens up and scuttles away, moving laboriously on at least one stunted leg. When the door rattles open the cat stops stock-still, feeling the vibrations in its jaw and stiffening tail, the leftovers of its winter coat bristling down its spine. But the man's voice rolls soothingly across the backyard, so the cat turns to face him.

"Hey, little ginger," he says. "Been a while, huh." The cat twitches one terracotta ear in response, and the man realises he has never heard the cat make a noise. It has always walked silently, never mewing or hissing at his son, never vocalising a complaint under his rough childish touch.

"I guess it's just you and me for a bit," he says. "Just you, and me, and my lovely morning coffee." He chuckles at the accidental rhyme. "What are you going to do when we're gone, ginge? You know I—we—sold the place, and somebody else is moving in."

The cat watches him. He watches the cat. For a few moments, they do nothing but watch each other with simmering intrigue.

"Sorry, mate, but it's part of the divorce deal," The man finally says. "I guess that's the way of things, though. Life moves at its own speed, right? Things change even when you don't want them to." The man pauses and watches the cat, wondering if it understands.

"What are you doing out there in the wet grass, kitty?" he says. "Come on, I've got some food here for you."

He goes to a plastic tub—the only furniture on the verandah—and pulls out a plastic packet. A handful of pebbles rattle onto a faintly outlined patch of decking, the ghost of an outdoor sofa. The man sighs. "Not that you need it," he says. "I remember when you were a skinny little thing sitting up on the fence watching us." The cat crunches a few pebbles.

"You know, little ginger, we talked about getting a cat of our own. Did you know you were Trevor's first word? You're not even our cat, and the kid says 'kitty' before he says 'mama' or 'dada'".

The man's deep, slow chuckle almost tricks the cat into purring. It has been out for hours hunting and exploring and is nearly tired enough to be overcome by the comfort of his voice. They go on like this until the food is finished, him talking and the cat crunching steadily until the food is gone. The man pours a few more pebbles on the floor but the cat ignores them. It turns as if to go but stops at the edge of the deck and sits. Something—several somethings—shiver the long blades and weeds, unshakable dew glistening in the muted sunlight.

The man sits on the bare deck with his back against the brickwork to watch the cat hunt for a while.

When the door sighs closed, the cat looks up towards the sound, but the man is out of sight in the dark house, obscured by another garden reflected in the glass. From the other side of the glass, the man watches the cat, knowing it's the last time they will see each other. He chuckles at the awkward way the cat high-steps through the dewy grass and leaps onto the back fence. He wonders what it means when the cat pauses and looks back; does the ginger interloper understand? *It's a big change for a cat*, he thinks, *to lose a surrogate family*. He decides that yes, of course the cat understands. It's an intuitive animal, if aloof. And he decides the cat will miss him. *Or maybe it's the other way around.*

The cat, weighing up its options, watches a young magpie preening on the verandah roof. Then the bird flies away, so the cat turns towards home.

VIII

An inconsistent spring wind blusters from every direction, but the sky is clear and the cat feels bold. Half-expecting to hear the man's voice or dodge the child's heavy strokes, the cat leaps from the fence, making for a patch of afternoon sun below. But something has changed. Fresh-cut grass tickles its belly and a heady, unfamiliar smell of fertiliser confuses its senses. The breeze scatters a cloud of acacia pollen in the cat's direction. Scrunching its face, fangs bared into a pained expression, the cat sneezes violently. The sound folds over itself, echoing, growing louder, resolving into a rapid snuffling. Instinct takes over and the cat freezes. Blood flows fast to all four limbs. Run—or fight. In all the backyards, all the comings and goings in the cat's everchanging neighbourhood, there have been plenty of near-misses with dogs. The cat knows what a designer dog's agitated snuffling sounds like. But the cat has never needed to watch for dogs in *this* backyard, so for a moment it stays prone, trying to locate the sound.

The cat backs towards the fence, hackles flickering in the breeze, as a pudgy sand-coloured dog rounds the house on four stubby legs, hopping more than running, panting with effort. It never has a hope of catching the cat. Before the dog is past the verandah, the cat is already on the fence. A man's voice wells up behind the dog, but it's not the same barrel-shaped man's voice that the cat is familiar with. Perched on the newly painted fence, it watches a strange man with a strange voice jog around the side of the house. From here it can stare down impassively while the obscene noise continues until the strange man finally quiets it.

"Stupid old cat," says the man with his scratchy voice that sets the cat on edge, "you should know better than to piss off a dumb little dog. Go on, get. Shoo."

The cat shakes its head and stretches. It watches the man take the dog by the collar back into the house. When the sliding door squeaks closed, the cat turns and walks purposefully along the fence towards the fibro house that will be knocked down soon to make room for the inevitable subdivision. But for now, it's home.

There are other backyards along the way, other constellations in the galaxy that the cat can observe from other fences, dropping down for a drink or treats if its timing is right. And if not, the cat will gradually make its way home. When it gets there, a man's gentle tenor will call the cat by name, goading it over the changing landscape to an unchanged house where it will be comfortable all night.

IX

The old cat never goes back.

Seep

Bethany Cody

Broken Hill, New South Wales 2009

Our daughter doesn't remember her birthday. Three weeks ago, we were gathered in the garden with the neighbours, holding our breath as Bella blew out her candles. We helped her cut the cake, Death by Chocolate, her favourite. Her cheeks bloomed a blotchy pink from the force of her sweet breath, her forest green dress wrinkled from playing with the neighbourhood kids and traipsing around the garden.

Five years ago, we moved to Broken Hill after a lifetime in the city. We wanted more for Bella:

wild, sunburnt land and open spaces for us to wander, breathe, away from the incessant noise of traffic, pedestrians, impatient drivers in sports cars. My husband secured his job as a logistics coordinator for the local mining company a month before we arrived. I spent the first few weeks in the new house, sorting through a horde of cardboard boxes teeming with our shit, playing Tetris in our tiny kitchen to relocate the plastics and crockery, eventually settling in.

Now Bella looks at me funny, after I ask her how it feels being so old.

'I'm three, not four.'

'Honey, your birthday was three weeks ago.'

She sourly disagrees with me.

'Honey—'

'No, it wasn't!'

I don't know what to say. She stomps away like a toddler, arms crossed.

It happens again a few weeks later.

We're in the kitchen. Ezra's watching me cook, swaying behind me to music only he can hear, his hands on my hips.

'She's incredible, isn't she?'

He nods into the back of my head.

'I can't believe she's three years old already.'

The illusory music stops, he stands still.

'What's wrong?'

He eyeballs me with concern.

'What?'

'Honey, her birthday was three weeks ago.'

I laugh at him.

'No, it wasn't.'

His eyebrows furrow.

'Are you feeling okay?'

'I'm fine.'

Bella comes through the kitchen doorway and hugs my leg.

'Mum, I feel sick.'

I sweep aside her brown, curly fringe and place my palm on her forehead. Her skin is warm, too cool to be a fever. I ask if she's eaten and suggest nibbling on some plain crackers.

'I'm not hungry.'

'Sip on some water then, you'll feel better soon,' I reassure her.

I fill her cup and watch her drink. She leaves and plonks herself at the foot of the couch to watch TV.

'Claire.'

'Mm?'

'Look at your phone.'

My wry smile fades as I scroll through my app. He's right. There are dozens of photographs I took of our little girl, rosy cheeks inflated, mouth pursed blowing out her birthday candles. All four of them.

How could I forget?

'Claire, are you feeling alright?'

I don't know what to say.

'Maybe you should take a nap, go to bed early.'

I take myself to our bedroom. Inside, it's cool and dim with the curtains drawn, turning the blue walls grey. I feel grey, cocooned in fog. Fraught dreams keep me hostage throughout the night.

***

Ezra's sipping coffee when I emerge in the morning feeling tired, strangely restless. He holds me while I eat a bowl of tasteless muesli.

'Maybe you should see the doctor?'

His shirt smells citrusy, suffused with the scent of his aftershave.

I call and get an appointment in the afternoon. The clinic is small and square, nestled between an intersection and a corner deli. Bird calls surround me as I walk along the uneven footpath to the clinic, passing by several old, well-kept houses with lush gardens.

Sitting in the consultation room they assure me I'm fine, if a little anaemic and tell me to, 'sit out in the sun a bit more every day,' while writing me a prescription for iron supplements.

When they offer nothing else, I grab my bag and head for the door.

***

At home, Bella shakes the bottle of pills around like a maraca, and eventually I have to take it off her when she tries unscrewing the lid. The muesli I had this morning repeats, comes back up and burns, so I check the fridge for something to nibble on and remember there's leftover birthday cake in the freezer. As I reach inside the frosty, crystalline interior, my hand hovers over the container. I picture Bella's green dress and before I can close the door I vomit, sending streams of gelatinous, acrid yellow onto the bottom freezer drawer and linoleum. It takes twenty minutes to clean up, and still the faint stink of bile hangs in the air.

At night, I tell him.

'I think I'm pregnant.'

Ezra is silent. I don't breathe.

'What?'

'What do you mean, *what?*'

'I don't understand.'

My silence forces him to explain.

'We haven't, y'know, done anything for a while, Claire. How is that possible?'

Reflux, anger, burns up the length of my throat until I burst. I sit up and spew profanities at him, calling him names, spitting in his face with the force of my hate.

'You are such an arsehole.'

I leave our bedroom to watch Bella sleep, half-hidden in the soft surrounds of her blankets and plush toys. She's a miniature of her father: dark hair, pale skin, infectious laugh. I remember how hard it was for us to get pregnant with Bella. She was the unexpected miracle a warm wind blew in through our bathroom window and over the positive pregnancy test in my trembling hand that Monday morning. She was the secret I kept for weeks until I couldn't and confessed to my co-workers, my friends, our parents, Ezra.

I fall asleep beside her bed, to the sound of her airy breathing.

***

In the morning, Ezra ignores me.

'Hey.'

He's at the sink, rinsing out his mug before heading to work.

'Ezra?'

He blows me off, stepping past me, and disappears through the front door.

I whisper an apology against the stained wood of the door, pressing my lips to the cool surface as the sound of his car pulling out of the driveway reverberates through the house. It's just Bella and me on our own today. She ignores me for a while as well, until I eventually coax her out of her funk and into my arms, holding her as I read from one of her favourite picture books.

She's at the age where she likes to eat dirt. As we play around the garden – she's my cub and I, her fearless mother lion – she picks petals from the flowers, digs in the ground for worms, squeals when she lifts up a pot plant to see slaters and snails unfurling and slithering out of the sunlight into cool darkness. It doesn't take long for the muck to get into her mouth, anytime my back is turned she smooshes it into her face, giggling when I catch her.

'Spit it out.'

She shakes her head, her eyes gleaming with amusement.

She's so clever.

'Spit it out, now!'

I take her to the outside drain and rinse her mouth.

We move inside for the day.

Ezra takes a while to warm up to me when he comes home. At first, I probe the tension between us, asking about his day, receiving silence. I ask about dinner, more silence. It isn't until after we've eaten that he comes to me on the couch.

He speaks into my hair, 'I'm sorry.'

'Me too.'

He sighs, unpleasant thoughts rushing from his mouth, disturbing the newspaper on the coffee table. 'It's getting really bad at work.'

'Oh?'

He falls back onto the plush fabric of the couch. 'The boss is riding my arse, pushing me to get these shipments out but…'

I rub his back in imperfect circles while he continues.

'Something's wrong.'

'What do you mean?'

'I don't know how to explain it.' His eyes are fixed on the TV. 'Everyone's acting weird, calling in sick all the time. The boss is being super shifty, hushed whispers behind closed doors. Nobody's telling us what's going on. Something just isn't right.'

I drape my arm across his chest. His heart pounds through the checked fabric of his shirt. I make it sound playful, 'How much coffee have you had today?'

'Just one, this morning.'

'Just *one*?'

He shrugs. 'Had a migraine, didn't feel like it.'

I make a noncommittal noise against his shoulder and glance at Bella, lazing on her belly in front of us as she watches commercials flash across the TV screen, which is smudged with fingerprints.

I tell him about the dirt, and he downplays my concern.

'Don't all kids do it?'

'Sure, but she looked hungry, like it tasted good.'

'Did she have breakfast?'

I ignore the accusatory tone and think back to this morning, to the bowl of bloated muesli that sat untouched on the countertop for hours while Bella scribbled in her colouring books, lying listlessly on the lounge room floor, a woeful wisp of her usual self.

'I don't think so.' I pause for a moment. 'What if she's sick?'

Ezra is slow to get to his feet, holding his side like my presence bruised him. His face is drawn, haggard when he stops in the doorway and says, 'She'll be alright. We'll keep an eye on her.'

***

Icy fingertips travel over our skin at night. Ezra pulls the quilt tight over his shoulders and hunkers down, leaving me to shiver and lose sleep. When I wake next, it's still dark outside, darker inside and I miss those nights under the full moon when everything is unusually bright.

'*Claire.*'

I glance at Ezra, still asleep.

'*Claire.*'

His lips are closed.

A pulse of something urgent moves through me.

Our room feels full, the air is thin.

I look at Ezra again: he still hasn't moved. Slowly I leave the bed, careful not to wake him. The hair on the back of my neck pricks up, but my hands are stiff at my sides. I can't will them to move, to soothe it.

The house is quiet, the street empty of light and sound.

'*Get out.*'

I turn towards the noise, the voice. The half-lit hallway greets me. As I turn again for the bedroom, a black mass passes in front of my face, fast and frigid. I follow it with my eyes, and there, in Bella's doorway, I see a woman.

Her face is pallid. Deep, venous wrinkles spread out from the centre of her ugly face like spider's legs. My stomach quivers, my pulse punches against a sudden tightness in my skin.

'Get out.'

Her mouth is black, missing teeth. There's no shape to the body beneath her ashen face. Darkness surrounds her, emanating from the toothless hollow of her mouth.

I open my mouth to shout, but before I can get the words out, the woman moves into Bella's room. The light flickers on. I run after her, feeling like I'm moving in slow motion. It takes twice as much energy, like wading through dark, arctic water.

From the doorway, I see Bella asleep in her bed, a yellow teddy bear tucked under the crook of her arm. I peer around the room and see nothing but the bright, cosy bedroom we built for her five years ago. The window is shut, locked. Her closet is empty. There's nothing but dust and a stray sock under the bed.

I don't know what to think.

'Oh, Bella...'

I lay beside her on the bed, quietly crying into her hair, waking her.

'Mum?'

Her sleep-thick voice pulls tears from deep within, draining me until the water recedes and I feel light again.

***

In the morning, I tell Ezra.

'I saw something last night that I can't explain.'

Confessing every horrid detail, I tell him about the woman in stops and starts. His face is still, unchanged. Anger rises in me, a hot, white ball of aggravated energy. It builds until I bite.

'Why are you looking at me like that?'

'I'm not looking at you like anything.'

'You think I'm crazy.'

'I think you're sleep deprived.'

Tears fall from my face to the floor below, misting my feet with saltwater.

'Don't cry, Claire.' He sighs, big and heavy. 'I don't know what you want me to say.'

I don't know what I want him to say either.

***

She comes back a few days later.

Searing afternoon sun burns across my face as I unclip our washing from the hills hoist. It's a sad thing, rusted around the bolts and wonky, tilting left. The breeze is cool, drying the sweat on my neck and lower back. The washing basket is heavy in my arms, the plastic cuts into my fingers and they sting from gripping the handle.

As I step inside the house, my grip falters and the basket tips, sending our clothes across the floor. I crouch down, putting aside the basket to gather up the fabric when a black shadow drifts across my line of sight. I glance up and see nothing. I look behind me, but the garden is empty, the side gate is closed. As my hand touches Bella's soft t-shirt, I see it among the tangle of clothes, a dark mass darts out and scampers behind the kitchen counter.

It's quiet.

Carefully, I step around the counter and peer down.

A crow with curious, pale blue eyes looks up at me.

It hops towards me, its head twitching left and right, its eyes surveying the room.

'*Claire.*'

Goosebumps sprout on my arms and I drop Bella's t-shirt.

'Claire?'

This time, it's Ezra's voice.

The bird is gone.

I turn and see Ezra standing in the doorway. The woman with the black mouth is behind him, impossibly tall, looming over my husband. Her eyes are sunken, glossy black wells streaming with dark fluid, running into her cavernous mouth, down her chin and onto the floor.

'What's wrong?'

He moves for me, and the woman vanishes.

'There was a bird. A-and then there wasn't a bird. It flew out of the basket and scared me and I couldn't find it, I–'

He hushes me, pressing me into him. He smells of sour citrus; sweet, but rotten. A wave of nausea surges up from the pit of my stomach and I pull away.

He brings me back in. 'You're okay Claire, you're alright.'

In the circle of his arms, a single drop of something small, dark and warm falls onto my arm. I watch it bloom outwards, its clear edges becoming undefined. It snakes down my skin, onto my shirt.

Blood.

'You're bleeding.'

He touches his nose. 'Shit.'

I sob into his chest.

'I'm okay.' He runs a hand under his nose, smearing the blood. 'We'll be okay.'

North Brighton, South Australia 2010

It seeps in through the pipes, the ground underneath our homes and into our water. We drink it, boil our spaghetti in it, shower in it, grow our fruit, herbs, flowers in it. It's in the air, brushing up against our clothes drying outside on the line, weaving through the cotton fibres, swirling above our homes, our unsuspecting heads. It's in every cell of our bodies, burrowing in at the most miniscule level like Bella had when I was pregnant.

At first Ezra thought I'd lost it, inherited something sinister from a distant relative, undiagnosed, swept under the ancestral rug. He took me to the hospital when I couldn't stop vomiting and they took my blood and bone marrow. A few days later, he collapsed at work and was diagnosed with dangerously high blood pressure. Gradually we grew better, stronger. Bella perked up again, gaining an appetite and weight. She stole my hospital snacks and burrowed her little body into my chest while we watched boring daytime TV we could hardly hear. Ezra stayed away most of the time, recovering at home. Though some days, when I could stomach it, he brought me flowers and frothy coffee from a cafe across the street.

At home we became neat freaks, washing our hands religiously with soap and hot water, drying our clothes inside the house. We smothered every inch of soil in the backyard with woodchips and each time Bella ran outside to play, I wrestled her back inside. Sometimes she'd burst into a pink-faced fit of tears and I'd distract her with books and toys and the promise of chocolate yoghurt. Ezra left his work shoes outside on the verandah and for a while we lived in our own insipid, reclusive bubble.

An investigation launched six months after my hospital stay ended in a record pay out by the mining company. We got a nibble, other families took their share and moved on. When it became clear it was exactly that, hush money, we packed up our life and moved.

We live a normal life again, south of Adelaide. Bella's fallen behind in her classes. Her doctor tells us she's experiencing developmental delays as a side effect of the lead. I'm back at work behind a counter in a sprawling mall in Tea Tree Gully. Ezra's sick of his new co-workers, but he's good at his job. We're thinking about getting a dog. Bella wants a cat, but I'm allergic so we haven't decided yet.

We take our medication as prescribed.

I don't tell them I still see her.

Nothing Is Motionless

Lydia Trethewey

Gerald's moustache is grey. He looks like his dad, like my dad, like all dads. I don't want to be a mother.

I pack the car in silence. Aeroplanes make diesel streaks above me, train carriages and highways filling out space. In the front yard is a palm tree, in the back yard is a palm tree, the neighbour's aspirations leak over the fence in faux-paradise aesthetic. It's hard to breathe here, inhaling other people's exhaust.

I'm exhausted because of the way the world shakes. I feel it, beneath my feet, my marrow a tuning rod. It's in the furniture and the sky, in the late night TV shows. It's over in America, and here, in the most isolated city on the planet. Everything trembles. I need someone to understand.

Gerald looks like a sea captain. Navy stripes would suit him, but his work uniform is a red polo shirt which makes his cheeks flush. He could pull off a pipe, if he tried. Like his dad, like my dad, like rich dads.

When people ask us why we don't have kids yet, Gerald looks uncomfortable, looks to me for guidance. I shrug and say, *I'm not even thirty yet.* And they smile, unsatisfied, and say *yes, Elena, but your husband's almost forty.*

I don't know how to make you better, Gerald says, in bed, in later, in sunken behind the eyelids.

And I know he means *I don't know how to make you* feel *better*, but I'm so caught up in the world's hurricane that it hardly makes a difference. All the small words that blow away, they're the ones I need to hear.

I finish folding my life into the backseat. The car is old, decrepit, with bumper stickers from previous generations.

My mobile rings, my manager's name flashing on the screen. I should be at the hotel now, making fresh beds, turning down rooms for travellers from more interesting lives. I don't answer, mute the phone and put it in the centre console.

The seat is worn, warm, and waits for wherever I need to go. South, I think, where the temperature drops. The trembling might be slower there, sound waves struggling through the colder air. Scattering further, maybe, but taking longer to reach my body, giving me time to adjust. I need to acclimatise to the world. Is it strange that after twenty-eight years I still haven't managed to belong anywhere?

Albany Highway is the name of the road I take. In Armadale it's double brick houses and shopping centres on the corner. There's a day care and a place where a bikie murdered a woman a few years ago, smashed her head in with a hammer. The vibrations are road noise, are tremors along a pendulum swinging me between here and there, through fluctuating levels of daydream. My reverie count is low. I have to reach escape velocity and burst out of this suburban grip.

Beyond the Perth metro, Albany Highway encounters bush. State forest, Noongar land, roadhouses with expensive fuel and fried food varnish. I travel through places with tenuous names, marks on a map.

Can I breathe yet?

Eucalypts line the sky, are poems with roots that have been here longer than me, outlasting the colonial invasion. There are trees in this country that are older than cathedrals, and when

Notre Dame was on fire, people online were angry that we were cutting those forests down, making room for slip-lanes.

I can feel the world through the steering wheel, through my palms, reading ley lines in my own skin. The car is an extension of my being, hybridised landscape, both present and absent. I feel the world shaking, and it's not the physical chattering of my teeth, not the asphalt winding tightly in my speedometer, it's the sense that matter moves and quivers and won't keep still. It's a thread pulled taut between everything and everything else, from which sound emerges. I hear it beneath the colour of my own flesh. It all trembles. I need to find someone who can understand this with me.

I go faster than I should, 115 then 120, back down to 90 behind a caravan, overtake at 130. One hour, two. On the fourth Gerald calls. I don't answer. I keep going on this single road, knowing I don't have to plan where I'll end up.

Albany is already sick of me, as I pull in behind the IGA, get bread and tea, finish this headache and pick it up again later.

There are holiday units all clumped together near the shore. I pay at the desk, get a key, collapse onto a bed with a seafoam doona that smells of moth's feet.

Gerald has called, and called, and why doesn't he realise that I've disappeared?

I don't yet realise I've disappeared. Will the cops come for me, a name on a missing person's report?

I call Gerald.

Elena? Where are you? I've been ringing and ringing.

His voice is sweating. I hear it drip onto his red polo shirt, stain the fibres. I picture his father-moustache and the stubble that already clings to his neck.

I have to be away for a while, I say.

What? What are you talking about?

I can't make the world stop.

That's not an explanation.

I know I owe him something, but the words aren't there yet, so I hang up.

I walk onto the beach, barefoot, lungs crystalline and full, and put my toes in the water.

The foam is white and makes me sallow.

The ocean goes on forever. There are whales out there, singing, mourning, being murdered. Albany was the place their carcasses were once dragged ashore, suffocating under themselves, bodies burning in lamps and powering ships, oil-slick nights hunting leviathans to skin them alive.

Blubber is the word. Meat. Animals becoming fire.

I walk, my ankles leaking feeling into the water, my jacket too thin to keep me warm. The waves here are still pissed off with history.

My thoughts are flensed.

The trembling is loud.

I can feel the wind. The ocean. Cthulhu. Phytoplankton.

The world's microscopic motions shunt me back and forth, but I can't fully grasp it without speaking it aloud. I don't have the names, the syllables. I need the vibrations from someone else's throat to be consonant with mine. The sound waves have to bounce back, received and sent.

There's a slight incline, a dune, and I can see a shack perched at the top, black beaten panels. Precarious gulls wheel about and disperse, white feathered flecks becoming ocean crests. Around me the beach is emptying.

People are evacuating the sand ahead of a storm.

In other parts of the world, on wrong days, the tide is sucked out suddenly, leaving dead fish flapping in over-oxygenated air. The ocean recedes into a single blue line, gone. Time seems to hold still, a surrealist landscape, marine life lost in a desert. Onlookers wander out to marvel at it all.

Then the water comes seething, smashing back, all at once, inescapable. A 747 jet-wave converting energy into destruction.

That's how a tsunami arrives: from a moment of wonder at the absurd.

I think about this as I walk across the beach, in the direction of the shack. Would I be one of those people, chasing the disappearing tide into the open arms of disaster?

Excuse me, I say, to a man all in black. He's a silhouette in an old painting, untouched by the silvering sky. He's walking briskly, in polished black shoes on wet sand.

Yes?

He turns, and I see the white collar. This man is owned.

Does someone live in that shack?

An evil woman. A sorceress. Don't go there under any circumstances.

I need to find someone who feels the vibrations of the world.

We have a service tomorrow, at nine am.

Thank you.

I continue towards the shack.

She's a hag, a she-devil. She killed her husband, the man shouts after me.

Within the chipped stoneware mug is a substance like lard, solid and slippery, smelling of brine. I look down at it, uncertain. The room tastes of castor oil.

Joan, the woman says. *My name is Joan.*

Old Joan

Saint Joan

Her lips peel back from narrow teeth. She gestures at the mug in my hands. *Well, go on then.*

She sits on the wicker couch, and I crouch on a dying Persian rug. The shack is small but doesn't feel it, a peripheral home carved out of a world where everything needs to be bought and sold.

What is it? I ask, sniffing the white lumps.

Whale milk.

There are lines of clay pots along the ocean-facing wall, nets not yet ghosts, a black diver's suit with a gash in one leg.

Go on.

Can you feel the world shaking?

Joan smiles, craggy, witchcraft scheming. *When you drink that, a portal will open on the ocean floor, and you'll fall through it into a world where everything is still.*

I lift the whale milk to my mouth and let it slide down onto my tongue, slurping soft butter out of the sea. It smells like liver and cream, glutinous, greasy, still too alive.

The sky outside is darkening.

Nothing's happening, I say.

Isn't that what you wanted?

I sit awhile and see. *No. I want someone to understand that the world trembles. Then maybe it will stop.*

Old Joan, witch Joan, laughs. *Blood shivers in your veins, thunder rattles the sky. The world will never stop shaking. Peace is the illusion of those who have given up.*

You're wrong, I say, and stand.

Joan, Saint Joan, ghost Joan, rises too. *My husband disappeared into the sea. One day that portal will open for me, too.*

I see the paraphernalia on my way out.

Outside, air as ice alights on my face. Standing on the dune peak, looking down, I feel raindrops on the back of my head, tiny splashes like bullets breaking the skin. Glowing clouds scud too fast over the waves.

I know that inside the shack, she drinks the milk, hoping it will open a hole in her brain through which she can disappear.

Raining now, in broken mirror shards. Here I am, at the edge of a continent.

If I stepped off this ledge, tumbled down into the sea, would my body continue the journey?

On the map I'd sink straight to Antarctica, a human ice block, archeologically locked into glacial rivers. I'd become pure and toe tagged in museum archives.

But the tides wouldn't do that for me.

I might get swept West and North, end up dashed against Madagascar, Sri Lanka or the Arabian Peninsula. No passport stamps required.

Or my death could spiral endlessly in the Indian Ocean centre, afloat on gyres of trash, a wasteland like any other, where fictional pirates build a new apocalypse.

Probably, definitely, I would just find my corpsed way to the ocean floor, consumed in pieces that break away, soggy bits of brain and sinew becoming parts of water, breathed in by sea-snakes and anemone and megalodon bones. That's all. Death and decomposition, owned at last by the biological and not the cartographic.

I walk back down to the beach, weightless on the compact ground.

On the main street of town, I see the priest through a cafe window. Warm, orange lamplight cuddles him. Puddles form on the bitumen road.

Through the swollen vessels of his eyes, and the intervening panes of glass, he sees me: a moment of recognition. As we stare at each other, my phone rings.

Where are you, Gerald asks, *I'm freaking out.*

I've just gone away.

'Just gone away' what does that mean? Elena, please, tell me where you are.

I've been gone for a while.

You were here this morning.

I've gone out to find myself.

pause

Elena, what the hell are you talking about?

The world is shaking and I need someone to feel it with me.

pause

Please come home.

I can't come home. I don't know where I am.

Elena, what—

I hang up.

Back on the unwarmed, seaside-holiday bed, facing a blank TV. The whale milk has left a rancid taste in my throat, a gummy, stuck sensation. It won't wash out.

When I was sitting on Joan's salt-scrubbed rug, inhaling its threadbare ruddiness, a memory slid into the back of my head, one that re-emerges now, through the textured walls and tiled floor.

I remember:

I was fourteen, on a camping trip at Moore River. My school friends and I all slept in a big tent together.

The nights were easy to elongate. We talked big and long and into the curls of each other's cochleae. We played spin the bottle, and there was nothing abnormal about a bunch of girls making out. Then someone flashed around a magazine of men and tween dreams and the moment was spoiled. They oozed over abs. I pretended to be interested.

Now some of them have girlfriends and wives, and I feel kind of rotten inside, like there was something I was supposed to realise but never managed to.

I want to lie down on my back again, beneath rivulets of rain on canvas, and feel the world shaking with friends who are as unsteady as I am.

The whale taste, murky and deep, is gone. The storm has settled with the night and pink clouds lie silky over morning.

I need to touch the sun, I decide. The vibrations aren't slower here, they're just sharper. North, to where the desert falls into the sea, that's where I have to go. I get in my car and drive.

Do whales have nipples?

I stop at an unnamed beach after not too long and stretch.

Grains of sand are atoms grinding against each another, and I slip through the spaces between them. Friction transferred from wind to waves to shore, liminal zones of ghost crabs disappearing into holes, snails leaving solid lines in their slow wake.

A moving column of water, Tiamat looks for Abzu, salt and fresh water intercourse becomes the origin of the world.

Their vibrations continue on.

Gerald is a fixture, like the city, embedded at the continent's western edge. I have to drive past Perth to get on top of it, to find the opening of the desert.

When I come in range of our house, only an exit away, my hands start to shake, and I know I can abandon this journey now. I can wind back everything that's happened, salvage this wreckage. I could live with Gerald, quietly but contentedly, beneath the transplanted palm trees. I could turn as grey as his moustache.

But I won't. I keep driving.

The car is shaky, past its use-by, like me.

It's getting warmer, and I realise that I'm going about this the wrong way.

What I need is to find someone who feels the Earth's tremble. And I can't do that from inside a car.

I pull over, not sure where, under shading eucalypts by a roadside petrol station. The sun is an asshole, leering at my exposed skin.

Attached to the station is a convenience store — torches, pool toys, ice-cream box — and I wander down its aisles, each one crammed with relics from the nineties, family road trip memories, still the same.

The cashier is a middle-aged woman with star-scarred arms and a bristling frown. I can almost hear her *hey, settle down now* growl. I buy a choc-milk, Masters, nostalgia, but there aren't plastic straws anymore. The woman hands me my change while staring out the door. Jimmy Barnes bleats in the background.

Not ready to be closed off again, I sit at one of the picnic tables on the shifting gravel edge. Road trains fill up from the diesel pumps. A car squashed with camping gear and kids pulls in, pulls out.

There's a message from Gerald on my phone.

I know what this is about. I understand that you're hurting. But please, come home so I can help you.

A skink runs across the blistering concrete.

My husband offers me passage, an outstretched hand. I delete the message.

I sit and sip my drink, soggy paper fibres sticking to my lips. There is stillness between the roaring engines.

Turning my head, I see a woman approaching, not from a car but from nowhere, rounding the building block. She's a desert apparition, a mirage. Her eyes are clasped on mine, and I stare silently with straw in mouth, sucking milk like a calf.

Her legs are bronzed, her arms hanging loose. She wears a mini-skirt, suggestions of pelvic bones and things below.

I have lot lizard suspicions, strangely, faintly hopeful.

Hi, she says.

Hello. I give her one more syllable than she gives me.

Where are you going?

Nowhere.

She smiles. *Where are you coming from?*

Also nowhere. Now I smile. *Can you feel the world shaking?*

Of course, she says.

My heart begins its movement.

Where do you feel it?

She looks down, lashes shading lenses, to the pit of her navel, to everything sliding along her legs. In my body.

Not in the ground? The air?

It gets outside eventually. But it comes from within.

Are you like me?

She blinks against the vicious sun, the quaking molecules of sky. My body is normal and hers is marginal. My problems are secrets, inward, circular, I hardly know if they exist, and I can't tell where they originate. She has real life stamped all over her.

The stranger looks at me with pity. *I doubt it.*

My desperate attempt to belong is silly, vain, almost contemptuous. I don't know anything about anything.

Ok, I say.

Move on.

This isn't about Gerald, though many of my thoughts begin with him. I'm not pregnant. My departure wasn't about the baby he wants or the miscarriage that never happened.

I didn't mean to lie, but it was convenient to say our hopes (his hopes) were blood in my underwear. I don't want to swell with other worlds. I don't want a child to swim through my amniotic sea.

The truth will follow eventually. Gerald is a captain, navigating the rolling surface of my dishonesty.

Do we come into this world across an ocean? And can you hear it, ear pressed to the pregnant belly as if to a conch shell?

White sperm and white whales and other things that seem to be related but aren't.

There are common myths, from ancient places, in which the world is formed from a woman's body. I wonder, are women allowed to form for themselves rather than for humanity? Are we allowed to make ourselves?

What is my cosmogony?

The world is dreamed, breathed, spoken into existence. Sometimes secreted, but from a woman is usually taken, her body the substance, she the material. How much culture is in biology, how many of our ontologies are just bad science.

At the mouth of the Murchison, where Tiamat meets Abzu, I stop. Tiredness has encircled my eyes, and I drive around town looking for a place to rest.

In the end, it's a cheap beachside motel with prickly grass and plastic fish on the walls.

Tourists are returning, with sandy feet and sunburnt shoulders, to big heaping plates of battered flake.

Some people are anadromous, breathing equally well in cities and country. They recline against any backdrop.

Sometimes I feel my emotions, and other times I just know that I have them.

Sometimes I fall in love with people who don't exist.

The best place to be alone is surrounded by other people. I know this is trite, obvious, asinine, but I ascribe to it anyway, because I don't really want to be alone.

I have a friend who lives in Exmouth, another full day's drive up the coast. She always seemed to know what was going on, what things meant.

I eat the bread from the Albany IGA for breakfast and get back into my car.

The ocean is there, always, even when it's not. After a few hours inland I find it, press my body towards the water. The wind is bracing, enlivens my dormant mood.

Perhaps instead of the distant, died-out mythologies that supply my imagination, I should try to learn about the indigenous stories of these places. An information plaque outside the motel had said that the Nanda people inhabited this land – ominous past tense – but I don't know much about the Dreaming, and I don't trust tourism signs to be sincere.

Keep going.

Along the highway are corpses like polyps, animals collapsed in on themselves. It's scary how quickly a kangaroo shrivels into skin, fur flecked with blood and inside-out. The landscape is so flat here, how could you not see it coming.

There are termite mounds punctuating the scrub, huge red domes rising like desert architecture, like old paintings of the tower of babel.

All the ants speak different languages.

There are too many hours to count. When I climb out of the car, dizzy, my legs shake.

The town of Exmouth is tiny and I'm an asphalt botanist, figuring things out through the pavement.

Gerald stops calling.

I don't want to be from a place but of a place. I don't want to be owed to other people but a part of them.

I haven't seen Steph in a long time.

I don't recognise her as she emerges through the unfamiliar people in the Ningaloo visitor's centre. Is that because my brain is already filtering out everything I don't need, preparing for starvation?

It's not that I don't trust my memory, but my memory doesn't trust me. I can't know what's important and what isn't. Neural trimming, housekeeping, cuts away all the things I try to keep, and the shadows of Steph's cheekbones, the shape of her walk, the way her voice pierces my reverie, these are already disappearing.

Hey, Ellie, she says, and wraps her arms around me. *It's good to see you.*

I didn't mean to come so suddenly.

I'm glad you're here.

There's another person here, beside her.

This is Alissa.

A shy smile, an averted gaze. Their fingers are interlaced.

How long have you two been together? I ask.

I don't ask them about the trembling world, because they might not understand yet.

Steph and Alissa are in the insular stages, where the rest of the world exists somewhere else.

The Ningaloo Reef is the biggest fringing reef on the planet, Steph says.

She takes groups out onto open water, to swim with the whale sharks.

Each whale shark has a unique pattern just behind the gills, like a thumbprint.

Steph imparts information like breathing.

You know, says Alissa, *human fingerprints aren't actually unique.*

That's reassuring, I say.

This is one of my favourite places.

Steph is wearing near see-through bathers and pointing out to the strip of white peaks.

The goggles fit tightly to my face, leave red welts that rise, stinging with the salt water. I breathe through a plastic tube, struggling to stay submerged. It's quieter underneath, but all my own movements are louder.

Brightly coloured scales, moray eels, giant clams with colourful gums clamped shut, all jumble together and pass beneath my bare thighs. A treasure-chest world unfolds, and I want to cry.

Over east the coral is dying, bleached white like bones.

The sky a vault, a ribcage, stars are punctured skin letting light flow through from some other place.

I sit beside the campfire, toes buried in the sand. Steph and Alissa sit beside each other, and when they ask me questions, I don't know how to answer.

I wake in the middle of the night, parched, deserted, and I need to tear the double gee out of my throat.

In my mouth the water is sand and blood.

In the bathroom, I stand in front of the mirror, and I'm not there. The figure is a skin-puppet, red creases where the sheets make me inanimate, one side of my face dead. I think, if I stare for too long, I'll leave forever. I woke but left the best part of myself asleep, my soul in dreams, and what stares back is not me, doesn't even look like me, ghostly gone and gone and empty.

Is it okay to live in dreams?

Dreams of soft lips and other clichés. Dreams of cunts on my tongue and scabrous, pubic, peeling back, my body burnt away. Dreams of sacrifice to the rising time, the changing climate, and crocodiles that are born different sexes depending on the temperature. Maybe I'm like those fish that switch their bodies when it's needed, I like dick, but I want women more. But if I act now, this desire might pass as soon, and I'll be more alone than I could reasonably stand.

Would I find the exit then?

Is a life spent in dreams well-lived if I feel happy there, and seldom okay anywhere else? I've been looking for my favourite places, but they don't exist, not in the sense that I could take someone to visit.

Is my reality unreality?

Is my sexuality so fluid that it could pour out of me all at once, and I would drown?

Steph and Alissa, my generous hosts.

Their love is twee, the kind that people had before the internet. They pile it up on sandcastles of poetry and kisses. They make out in the corners of the house when they think I'm not there. They fuck and try to hide it, but they take too many showers.

I hoped we could hear the world trembling together, but they only hear each other.

And it's insufferably, selfishly, uncharitably wrong of me to think this way. They're just people, who care about each other, in a way I don't know how, and they fight for it, against a tide of vicious commenters who exist somewhere in the murky edges, in the mangrove roots. They love despite the words of bigots who hate them obliquely. They live in defiance of disgust.

I'm just a lonely, bitter outsider terrified at the onset of suburbia.

I just want to fuck a woman.

I just want to love anyone.

I just want. I just need someone to understand.

A message from Gerald: *I love you.*

I have to go, I say.

The downturned edges of Steph's mouth are deliberate exercises of sincere emotion. She has a deep well of feeling but there's a disconnect in her brain, so her expressions don't change automatically. *You only just got here. Why not stay a few more days, if you've got nowhere else to be? It's manta ray season.*

I can't. I have to keep moving.

I never asked her if she could hear the world.

Sea snakes breathe through their skin.

I'm gone again, temperatures rising, steering wheel molten. My palms blister, life line unclear.

What happens if I run out of money and haven't found myself yet?

The roads are gaining orange, the sky blue and forever. It's winter but it's thirty-five degrees. Engine light flickering.

All my continents are separating, and as they do, tsunami vengeance rises. I summon the deep, the beyond and beneath. I'm carved from it. We all are. The fear is that we might connect again, not to each other, but to those shards of weirdness that sometimes pierce reality.

Do they keep us apart?

The water rises and boils away the sun
the earth shakes

the sky shakes

my core shakes

shakes me open.

I break down between Karratha and Port Hedland. The car won't start.

Nothing here but spinifex, too far from water, and I'm desiccating with the roadkill.

A 4WD, hopeful, dusted red, can't jump start me.

He's young, has a wiry beard and almost-dreadlocks. There's a six-pack beneath his shirt, and another on his backseat.

After too much time in the sun, he offers me a lift instead.

This thing's dead.

Okay.

A rusted carcass on the roadside.

It's ok, I'm not a serial killer.

That's exactly what a serial killer would say, but I'm beyond worrying about my safety. I might as easily die of exposure.

I'm Jonah.

Elena.

Vance Joy on the radio.

Where you heading?

Wherever.

Broome?

Sure.

I might be passively suicidal, based on the Emmengard scale.

I'm a tattoo artist, says Jonah, staring ahead through the windshield. *Taking some time to travel a bit, before uni starts again.*

Going the whole way around the country?

Trying to. How 'bout you? What do you do?

I don't do anything, anymore.

He laughs, lighting up his eyes. *Just travelling?*

Not really. Just looking.

Looking for what?

I shrug. *The world quivers. It won't stop, and I can't stop moving.*

I get you. I have ADHD, so my brain literally doesn't switch off. I'm always on.

That must be hard.

It's like, there's the executive brain, and the default brain, and the default brain is like background noise. It's the one that wanders away. Most people can switch it off. I can't. Best I can do is turn it down.

Dolphins only rest one half of their brain at a time, so they don't really sleep. They're continuously awake, active.

Steph tour-guiding inside my head.

That must be exhausting, I say.

Oh yeah. But it's also just how I am. I'm a chronic daydreamer.

Who says dreams aren't reality?

Gerald sends another message:
Do you still love me?

Of course I do, of course I do, of course I do, of
course I do of course I do of course I do of course
I do of course I do of course I do of course I do
of course I do of course I do of course I do of
course I do of course I do of course I do of course
I do of course of course of course of course of
course

of course of course
of course

I just don't love myself.

My dreams hurt now.

A day and a half gets us to Broome.

We spend the intervening night asleep on the soft shoulder, me foetal-curled in the backseat with the beer, Jonah in a tent under the stars.

The dirt here has a name: pindan. It's brightly pigmented, orange, red, solid with little shimmers of heat disturbing the air. It drops off suddenly into the ocean, azure, turquoise, clear.

There are roundabouts and cyclists. I see a boab squatting outside a car dealership, its bulbous trunk struggling to fit between the sidewalk and the seedy advertisements.

Jonah drives us to Port Beach past industrial silos, along bitumen roads which melt like magma into the bush.

Raptors circle above, clusters of them, more wings than I've ever seen at once. Kites, buzzards and sea eagles, waiting to pick off the lifeforms that crawl about below. They join the purple and blue squiggles scrawled across my eyeballs.

The pier is haphazard, thrust out towards the horizon, hung with fences and wires and places to tap your authorisation card. We pull off before the gates, into an empty carpark connecting two buildings. The ocean is on both sides.

There's a restaurant here I read about, Jonah says.

I'll shout you lunch. It's the least I can do.

We sit outside and pick apart fried fish with our fingers.

A tanker lurks on the horizon.

As we eat, we watch the vessels berthing.

Is that a cruise ship? I ask.

It seems too small, but the surface is polished, white and promising.

Looks like a superyacht. You know, like millionaires have.

I think he means billionaires.

I've always been afraid of the ocean, I say, wiping chip grease onto my shorts.

Really?

In a way. I might be scared of the unknown.

You know how you said that the world quivers?

Yeah. It's like an endless trembling that goes through everything.

You know it's inside of you, right?

It's not – it's in the air, and the stars.

Jonah laughs. *No, what I mean is, it's both. It's in the world, but also inside you. That's why you notice it. When the two align.*

I don't feel very consonant with the universe.

And yet you keep talking about how everything is strung together.

I say goodbye to Jonah in the carpark, and walk down steps that become stones, onto the sand.

A thousand tiny crabs greet me, jewel blue domes on upright legs, digging. Their holes perforate the beach. They only appear in movement, when I get too close, skittering away. When I stop, arms hovering like a burglar, they cease to be, and I can't see them against the glistening rivulets of water. The world only exists when I shake my eyes back and forth.

My skin abrades with lost granules which I carry away from their home. I relocate the beach in my socks.

I want to kiss her
    We're sitting outside a café
    In Perth
    She laughs and says, who are you
    I don't know
    Interrogation about my romantic history
    You're not really bisexual then
    I can prove it
    It's too late for that

My ex nihilo sexuality

Living daydreams

The pier itself is closed, a sign warning of spilled oil. A woman with leathered skin leans against the chain-link fence, smoking.

She sees me watching her.

Hey, she says, the word curled in beckon.

I redirect my steps to her, from nowhere in particular.

She blows out a cloud of smoke, cumulus blue eyes. *You a backpacker?*

I guess so. How could you tell?

You look like shit. Ragged.

Oh.

The lit end of her cigarette is an amber hole punched through the space between us.

You know how to fold bedsheets? She asks.

Yeah. I work in a hotel.

She raises an eyebrow.

Used to work in a hotel.

Married? She looks at the ring on my finger.

Barely. I'm not much of anything, anymore.

You want to get out of this place?

The inside of the superyacht is like the first class section of an aeroplane, opulence constrained by function. The chairs are white, everything designed around the circle, the curve. The rooms are sparse but neat.

Bernette, tobacco sourness clinging to the fibres of her uniform, shows me the crew cabins. Bunk beds with the same blanket pattern as the room in Albany.

Don't underestimate the amount of work you'll have to do. You'll likely be doing laundry all day every day, until we get to Bali.

How long will that be?

She shrugs. *Six to ten days.*

I can feel the ocean travelling up to us through the hull.

I see a container ship through the porthole window, so far off it seems not to move.

Steph is soap-boxing my thoughts again:

We don't often think of it, but big ships cause sound pollution beneath the water. Whales get stressed out, and then they stop breeding. It's like a ceaseless grinding in their poor soft brains.

Cthulhu is down there with the whales, unspeakably larger than them, where the bottom of the deepest trench inverts and becomes a mountain on top of which the gods sit.

Giant squids fight with sperm whales, their tentacles finding all the vulnerable places. Ancient hentai. But when the whales wash ashore and you slit their bellies open, thousands of smaller squids come rushing out. Whose fault is that.

I can't find the origins of those infinite insides and outsides.

The laundry smells of soap and salt. I'm here for enough hours to forget who I am. The phone network is out of range, no signal coming through.

To say I'm coming apart at the seams is to assume I was stitched together in the first place.

I wonder if people have been fucking on these sheets.

At night I masturbate, thinking of Bernette, my mouth stuffed full of pillow. She kisses me with ash-tray lips. She's desirable not because I like her, but because she's there, and I think she's lonely too. She's not afraid of open water.

While I work, skin cells puckered from detergent, from contact with the parts of people that flake away in the night, semen stains, I fantasise about a future.

I introduce Bernette to my parents. They're surprised, but supportive. We move into an old townhouse in Fremantle, near the port. We hold hands and know each other's signals. I slide an arm around her waist. She quits smoking. We're a couple, and not just an artefact of sex.

Things I know will never happen, so it's not cheating to spin them out inside my head, live them there.

I don't notice the bites for several days. Tiny calderas of blood and spice in droplets down my legs. I scratch them until I rupture and then keep going, mosquito memories drunk on me.

I could go anywhere on this boat and still be alone. I'm exposed, the cabin door without a lock. Inebriated moments along the corridors.

I heard a rumour that pods of male dolphins will harass a female until she passes out from exhaustion, and then gang rape her. These are ideas the guests entertain themselves with, claiming fully yes, or fully no, to the truthfulness of anything.

What was Jonah saying?

If the trembling is inside me, I'll never escape it. But if the vibrations link me to the world, I can exist anywhere.

So why can't I connect with other people.

Six to ten days later…

There are palm trees, and they actually belong here. But it's not paradise.

I guess I expected my old life to be shed as we docked, like skin blown away in the Indonesian breeze. How far do I have to go to strip my history off, to forget what I've done and what I am. My fears cling on, eat through my heart like slimy maggots, leave trails of the people I've hurt.

I miss Gerald. It's strange, because the world is still shaking, and it's inside me now too, funnelled in through Jonah's words. There were so many guests on board the yacht, but I didn't get to ask any of them if they suffered from ennui, if the trembling world was pointlessness incarnate, was the insignificance of an individual caught in an indifferent milieu.

My cabinmate didn't speak English, and I can't speak Filipino.

The sand is dirty. Tourists float in pristine pools, pretending the ocean isn't there. It's full of trash and buoys and boats, brown encrusted ropes, anyway.

I sit at a plastic table, eating a plate of chicken and rice. The superyacht is in the distance now, like so many places.

There's a sweet smell of fruit putrefying, a ground coating of tiny seed-splatter.

Dogs with protruding hip bones, scraps of fur missing around pinkish lesions, dash along the beach, sniff for fish and food. A man is raking up seaweed and burying it.

My body aches, my eyes exhausted, deadbeat sore feet near collapse.

Planes appear across the sea with their noses tilted upwards, anticipating the ground, fuselages lit by the sun, the undersides of their wings tinged a deep grey. They come from Perth, from Melbourne, from all over. People putting punctuation marks in the monotony of their daily lives. They arrive every five minutes and don't stop.

I finish my dinner, walk along the backs of resorts and restaurants, a concrete path beside the beach. The clouds are lit from beneath by a vague, fluorescent yellow glow.

I hear a familiar accent, Aussie but not Ocker. This woman is younger than me, pale and small, gathered up with her feet pressed flat on a reclining chair.

She's talking to herself, out loud, muttering over a notepad. I stop and watch her.

Visitor effluence, affluence, transgressor invasive species, she says. Her eyes follow her pen across the paper. Something, some kind of metaphor, something. Eighty percent of the island's income is tourism.

She looks up, sees me standing there. I'm slightly askew from weeks of non-stop movement.

What? she says, folding her notepad against her chest.

Nothing.

You're staring at me.

Is that a problem?

She frowns. *It's rude to stare.*

Why? Seeing is the basic unit of human connection. It comes before touching.

Are you coming onto me?

No.

It sounds like you are. Creep.

When you see someone, the light that has touched them and bounced off touches your retinas. So, they're touching you with themselves. That's how you see them.

You're fucking insane. She gets up, legs unscrunching. There's a tattoo of a stingray on her ankle.

I might be, I say. I don't know yet. What are you writing?

She pauses. An essay. About tourism.

Why do people come here?

She glances around: at men with bare chests, curly black hairs offered to the sinking light, at women wearing swimsuits and strappy tops drinking and breathing full. *Why did you come here?*

I needed to escape.

From what?

Myself.

She shakes her head. Fucking crazy bitch.

As I watch the young woman walk away, notepad clenched in fist, I realise something: I'll never find someone who can explain me to myself.

In the end I have the conversation inside my own head, a valid reality, to make it real The beach is junked with people, but they've got their own worlds to deal with.

So I say:

Elena, what are you doing here?

I'm seeking myself. I'm trying to escape myself. I don't know who I am

You're agitated, terminally restless

The world is trembling and I can't shut it out

But you're trembling too, within it. Do you want to stop?

If I stop, I'll die. There's so much more I want to do

So, you're scared of settling down. But you're also worried you won't be able to settle down, even if you tried, because of this internal restiveness.

I'm dissatisfied with my life. Scared of a slow suburban stagnation. I'm exhausted by the shaking, but the idea of being still is terrifying. So, I won't ever be happy. It's a no-win situation

But you enjoy being alive. You're full of your own worlds

It's so loud. I can't see through it

What is it?

I don't know. Myself. There's too much me, inside my head. It's interfering with everything. It makes things complicated

It's your life. Your inner world is part of reality

No

It's the one you prefer to inhabit. And that's okay

But I can't just live internally. I need someone to understand, to make the things I feel real

Then say it. Out loud. Speak this all into existence

I don't have the vocabulary. I think I've lost my sanity, with all the words that might have described it. There's just no space left, for me to be who I am, who I want to be

You need to be honest with yourself. And other people. About who you are

The world shakes, and I'm shaking

Nothing is motionless

But what if I stopped somehow? I might stay still forever. Then what if I needed to move again?

I don't think you'll stop. I don't think you can

In that case, if I'll always feel these vibrations, how can I function as a regular person?

Why would you need to do that?

Because that's the way it should be. The way I should be

Why?

I've pretended for so long to be normal. It's too late to do otherwise

Why?

Because if I come out now, if I show my true self, people will get hurt. To be myself is to sacrifice others

Is it?

I don't know

You want someone to understand you, but you refuse to say who you are. That's why you're so shaken up. That's why everything is overwhelming

I have to keep moving

Don't run

I have to

Don't

I can't stop

Listen to yourself

I can't

It'll be ok. You'll be ok

Please, understand me

You need to talk to someone

There isn't anyone

There is. Someone who knows you

I'm alone

You know who it is

I do

So talk

I can't

You can

I need to talk to someone who knows me

I pick up my phone. The battery's almost dead.

The ocean is black, an endless expanse melding with the sky.

Gerald's voice is grey, like himself, like no one else. But he doesn't hang up.

Contributors

BETHANY CODY is an Adelaide based, visually impaired writer of short stories and poetry. Her words appear in Voiceworks Magazine, Yellow Mama Webzine and InDaily Poet's Corner.

AMANDA JAYNE is an emerging writer based in Sydney. Her work has appeared in *Litbreak* and is forthcoming in *The Bitter Oleander*. She studied comparative literature at Oxford University and is working on a novel.

VASCO PIMENTEL is a 26-year-old writer and creative writing student at Curtin University. Based in Fremantle, this is his first published work in Australia. His work has also been published in the *Student Gallery Magazine* in the UK.

MORGAN RILEY is a 29-year-old writer from Western Australia, currently living in Copenhagen. He is fascinated by the way people interact; with each other, with their own inner multitudes, the world around them or their loved ones.

LYDIA TRETHEWEY is a visual artist and author living and working in Perth, Western Australia. She teaches visual art at Curtin University.

Editors

DENIZ AGRAZ is a bilingual writer based in Sydney. Having arrived in Australia from Turkey as a teenager in the late 90s, Deniz's writing regularly draws on the experiences of migrants. She is currently media officer at the Institute for Society and Culture and Western Sydney University. Deniz's writing has been published in *Meniscus Journal*, has appeared in *ABC Life* and *SBS Voices*, Fairfield Museum and the Finishing School Collective. She was shortlisted for the 2019 Deborah Cass Writing Prize.

Born in Queens, raised in Ecuador, and now living on unceded Dharawal land, **ELIZABETH MORA** is a writer and cultural worker entangled in the ambivalence of time, place and identity. She is an editor of *Drylight,* the University of Sydney Education and Social Work Society Journal. In 2019, she was a participant of Citizen Writes, a creative writing program developed by Carnival of the Bold and Diversity Arts Australia. Her work has been performed at independent arts events and published by the Australian Multilingual Writing Project, Sangre Migrante, Honi Soit and University of Sydney Press.

EMMA WORTLEY has a background in academia and has published papers on children's and young adult literature (the subject of her PhD thesis) in various journals. Her reviews, stories and poetry have appeared in *Voiceworks*, *Southerly*, *Going Down Swinging*, *Paper Crown Magazine*, *textLitmag*, *Scintilla Magazine*, *Scum Mag* and episodes of the *Story Club* podcast.

Spineless Wonders publications are available in print and digital format from participating bookshops and online. For further information about where to purchase our print and ebooks, go to the Spineless Wonders website:

www.shortaustralianstories.com.au